If You Can Read Music,
Thank Guido d'Arezzo

Do Re Mi

If You Can Read Music, Thank Guido d'Arezzo

Susan L. Roth

in association with

Angelo Mafucci

Houghton Mifflin Company ◆ Boston 2006

To ETL, who taught me to read music;
to JR, who taught me to sing

www.houghtonmifflinbooks.com

The text of this book is set in Historical.
The illustrations are collages made of papers from all over the world,
including many from Italy.
All photographs were taken by the author in Arezzo and in Pomposa.

Library of Congress Cataloging-in-Publication Data

Roth, Susan L.
Do re mi : if you can read music, thank Guido d'Arezzo / Susan L. Roth in association with Angelo Mafucci.
p. cm.
Summary: For many years, Guido d'Arezzo, a young man from Tuscany,
has imagined that his system of lines and spaces
can be used as a written language of music and he is determined to make his ideas work.

ISBN 0-618-46572-3 [hardcover]

1. Guido, d'Arezzo——Juvenile fiction.
[1. Guido, d'Arezzo——Fiction. 2. Music——Fiction. 3. Musical notation——Fiction.]
I. Title: If you can read music, thank Guido d'Arezzo. II. Mafucci, Angelo. III. Title.
PZ7.R737Do 2006
[E]——dc22
2005003811

ISBN-13: 978-0-618-46572-9

Manufactured in China
SCP 10 9 8 7 6 5 4 3 2 1

$17.00 U.S.
$22.95 CAN

If you can read musical notes, you can sing any song or play any piece.

But musical notes have not *always* been here. Long ago, songs were memorized. If songs were forgotten, they were lost forever.

Thanks to one man, Guido d'Arezzo, music now can last forever.

• • • •

Jacket art copyright © Susan L. Roth

wledgments

• • •

k, my friend Angelo Mafucci introduced
nths that followed, Angelo and I walked
any times. A renowned scholar of Guido
ngelo Mafucci discovered the landmark
n The National Archives in Florence.
, he continues in Guido's steps one
ucci has been *my* "maestro" as well
Guido himself, for this book.
to di Arezzo, Archivio di Stato di Firenze,
anuele II di Arezzo, Provincia e Comune
Carla Aretini, Monsignor Alvaro
manducci, Pam Consolazio, Nancy and
esswell, Ardito Croci, Enrico Fadda,
ssa, Marco Giuliani, Olga R. Guartan,
Grazia Mafucci, Judy O'Malley, Silvia
r, Karen Riskin, Marco Sofianopulo, Jill
, as always, AAAH, JR, ETL.

Foreword

by Angelo Mafucci

Angelo Mafucci, born and raised in Arezzo, holds degrees in musicology (University of Florence) and in singing (Conservatory G. Tartini, Trieste). In addition to being a teacher of music and a choral director, he is the founder of Centro di Ricerca e Documentazione Musicisti Aretini.

• • • • •

This book stands proud and tall to honor that great man, that deserving, justly named "Father of Music," Guido d'Arezzo. With Guido d'Arezzo's short but deliberate pen strokes, music was transformed for the ages. From the moment of his epiphany, to present times and forever after, we who hear music (and we who can read music) must thank Guido d'Arezzo.

For all of time, there was music. Music has shared its origins with the oldest of civilizations. Without a valid writing system, music could exist only in the present tense. Unlike other arts, music left us no legacy before it was written. And so it languished in history, waiting for its "savior." Ten centuries ago, Guido d'Arezzo gave all of us one of the most important, enduring links to the history of humanity. Guido d'Arezzo and his method of musical notation, a method as simple as it is still effective, changed the role of music everywhere and forever. By enabling music to live beyond the moment, Guido d'Arezzo immortalized it.

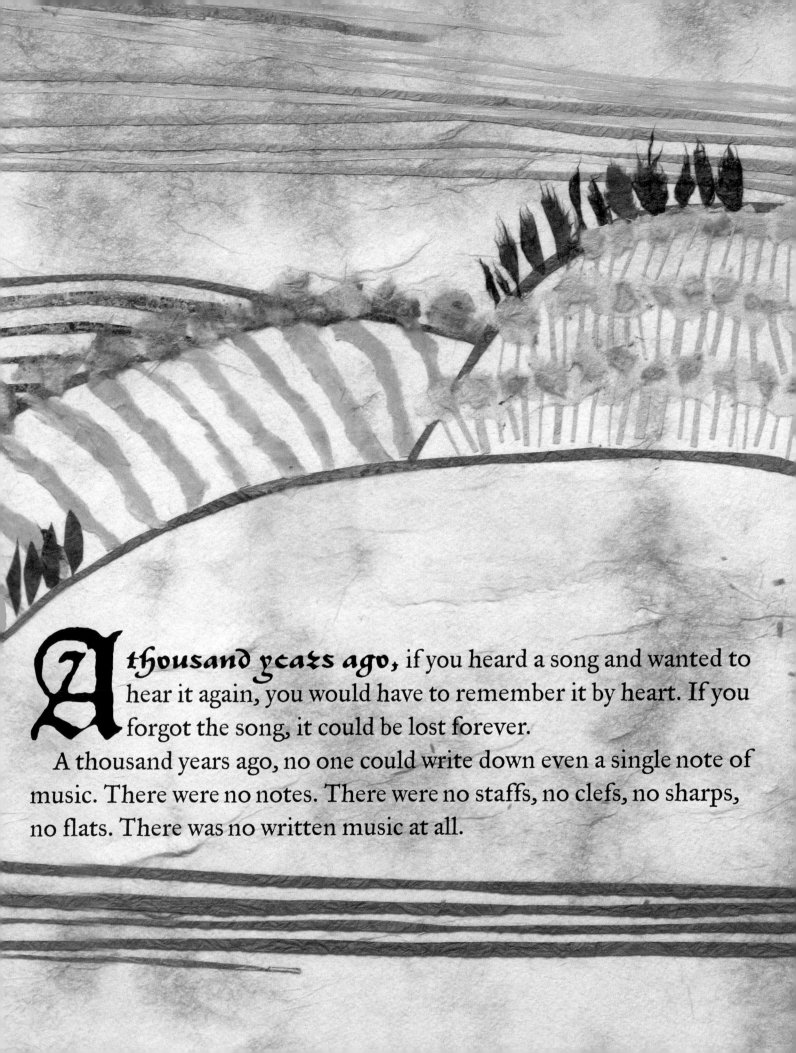

A thousand years ago, if you heard a song and wanted to hear it again, you would have to remember it by heart. If you forgot the song, it could be lost forever.

A thousand years ago, no one could write down even a single note of music. There were no notes. There were no staffs, no clefs, no sharps, no flats. There was no written music at all.

A thousand years ago, in a small city in Tuscany, Guido of Arezzo learned to sing by rote like all the children in the choir. The choirmaster sang a song, and the children repeated the song they heard. When someone needed a reminder, the choirmaster had to sing the song all over again. There was no way to read the sounds of a song like words in a book, because only the *words* of a song could be written. Words alone are not enough to keep a song alive forever.

The thought of writing down the *sounds* of a song slipped into Guido's head when he was still young. Others had tried to do this before, but no one had ever found a way. The thought stayed with Guido as he grew into a man.

Sometimes Guido tried to explain how easy it would be to learn to sing if only music could be read instead of memorized.

"What's wrong with memorizing?" asked Guido's teacher. "This is the way my father taught me to sing."

"Maybe it's not the only way," said Guido.

"Nonsense!" said Guido's teacher. "All day long I teach children to memorize their songs. What would I do all day if children could learn songs without me? Everything would change."

The musicians of Arezzo were not ready for change.
But Guido was ready. He said goodbye to his friends
and went to live with the Benedictine monks in Pomposa.

Again Guido tried to explain how easy it would be if only music could be read like words in a book.

"We already know how to sing," said the monks in Pomposa. "We love our music the way it is."

Brother Michael stood right next to Guido. He was the only monk who was really listening.

"So I could make up a song and write it down," he said, "and you could read it and sing it before you hear it? It *would* be like a book. *Anyone* could sing it if the music could be written. Think of that!"

"Exactly," said Guido.

"The choirmasters won't have anything to do anymore," said Brother Michael.

"They'll have *different* things to do," said Guido.

Guido began to write on parchments with his quill and ink even before his thoughts were clear. Sometimes he tried to explain what he had written to Brother Michael. Brother Michael praised Guido when what he saw was clear. He complained to Guido when what he saw was not.

Guido collected more letters and numbers and symbols than he knew how to use. His collections filled his room. His collecting filled his years. But how could he put them together? What should be included? What should be left out?

Guido thought about writing down the sounds of songs during his lunches and vespers, his late nights, his walks in the woods. He thought during homilies and lessons. He thought while planting in the garden, comforting the sick, mending the monks' robes. Even when he was busy teaching children to sing, and even when he himself was singing, Guido was always thinking about a written language for music.

Bit by bit, Guido began to build his musical system. But how could he put all the pieces together in a way that someone else would ever be able to understand?

Guido shut his eyes and held his head.
"You almost have it now," said Brother Michael.

"NO, I DON'T!" said Guido. He pounded his hand on the table.
He put his head down and started to cry. "I just can't do it," he said.

"Guido," said Brother Michael, "every day you get a little closer to the answer. You can't give up now!"

And then Guido had his epiphany.

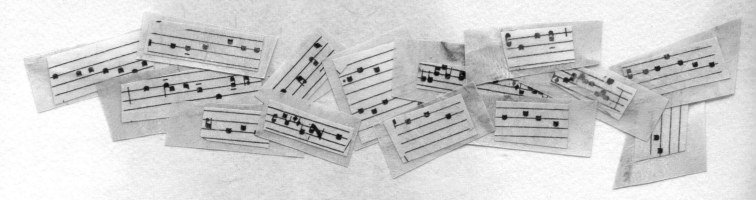

Guido organized his thoughts onto fresh parchments. Brother Michael was the first to see.

"Thank you for having faith in me," said Guido.

"I only listened while you worked," said Brother Michael. "Soon everyone else will listen, too."

But the other monks in Pomposa still were not ready to listen.

"We *like* the way we sing our songs," said the other monks. "If you want to write, write a story. If you want to read, read a book. If you want to sing, sing the way you were taught. Leave us alone, Guido. Maybe it's time for you to go home."

And so Guido decided to go back to his first home, back to Arezzo.

"I'll write you letters," said Brother Michael.

"I'll send you songs," said Guido.

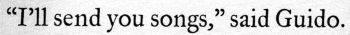

Guido sang his way back to Arezzo.
"Guido's back!" said his old friends. Everyone had missed him.
"Welcome home, Guido," said Teodaldo, the new bishop.

Teodaldo asked Guido to become master of the children's choir.

"I'll do it," said Guido. "And I'll teach the children to read music. *They* will prove to everyone that it *is* possible."

"Say that again," said Teodaldo. "What in the world are you talking about?"

"Look," said Guido. He held out his hand. "Pretend my fingers are lines. Don't look at my thumb. What do you see in between my fingers?"

"Nothing but empty spaces," said Teodaldo.

"Right," said Guido. "There are lines *and* spaces. Pitches go in order, from low to high. Each pitch has its place, either on a line or in a space. These are the pieces of the puzzle."

"Go on," said Teodaldo.

Everyone was listening now.

"Go on!" said the others. They had begun to understand at last.

Guido took a parchment out of his bag.

"Here is a song you cannot know," he said, "because I composed it. I've written it down. No one has ever seen it or heard it, except for the words, which come from an old poem. Remember that each line and each space has its own unique pitch. All right. Let me hear all of you sing it together!"

Teodaldo and the others *read* Guido's music. They *sang* his song!

"Bravo!" said Guido.

"Bravo, Guido!" they said.

Guido did teach the children in the choir to read music. Soon all the world was listening.

When the pope learned how to read music, he invited Guido to move to Rome. Guido was pleased to visit, but even the pope couldn't persuade him to move away from home again.

"I am Guido of Arezzo," said Guido d'Arezzo.

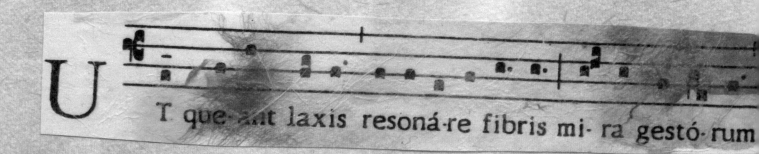

UT que-ant laxis resoná·re fibris mi· ra gestó· rum

And, a thousand years later,
that is how he is still known.

mu-li tu- ó- rum, sol-ve pollú- ti lábi- i re- á-tum, sancte   Io- án

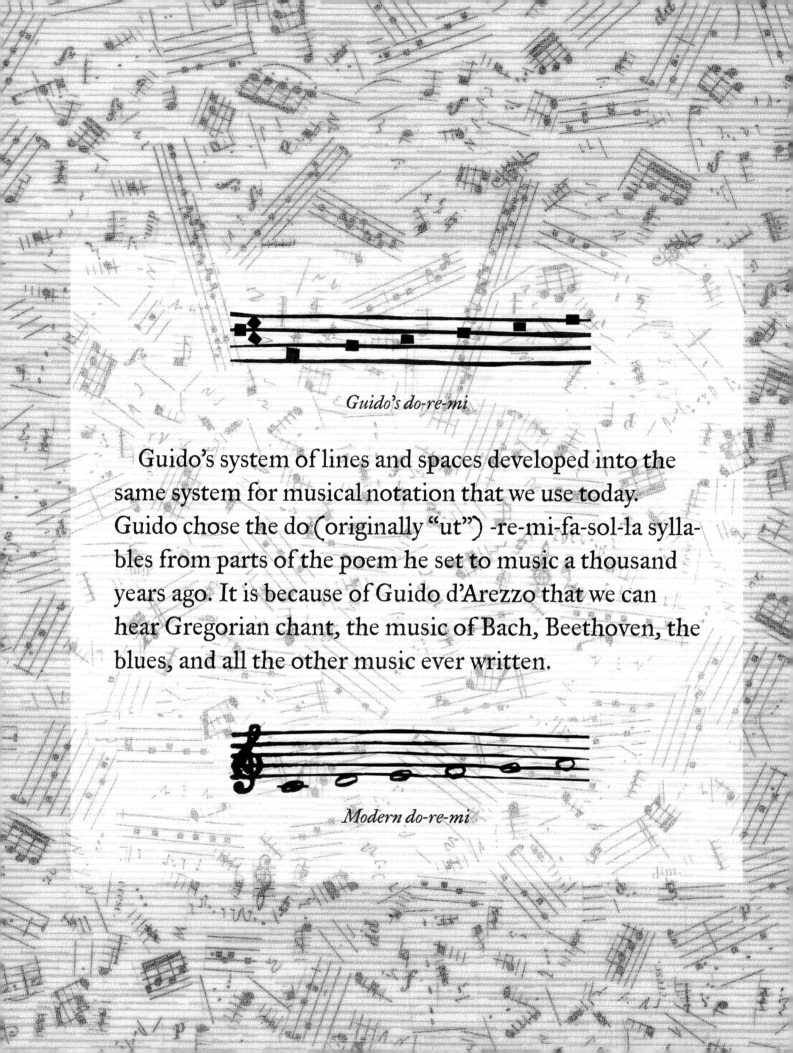

Guido's do-re-mi

Guido's system of lines and spaces developed into the same system for musical notation that we use today. Guido chose the do (originally "ut") -re-mi-fa-sol-la syllables from parts of the poem he set to music a thousand years ago. It is because of Guido d'Arezzo that we can hear Gregorian chant, the music of Bach, Beethoven, the blues, and all the other music ever written.

Modern do-re-mi

Glossary

CLEF: a sign placed on the musical staff to show what pitch is represented by the lines and spaces. (𝄞) treble clef (𝄢) bass clef

DO-RE-MI-FA-SOL-LA-TI-(DO): syllables used for tones of the scale.

FLAT: a character (♭) indicating a note that is a half step lower in pitch than the note named.

NOTES: characters (♩♪♫♬) in music used to indicate the pitch by their positions on the staff and the duration of a tone by their design.

PITCH: highness or lowness of sound.

RHYTHM: movement of sounds marked by recurrence of accents.

SCALE: a series of musical tones going up or down in pitch according to a specified scheme.

SHARP: a character (♯) indicating a note that is a half step higher in pitch than the note named.

STAFF: the five horizontal lines (▤) on which music is written. (Guido's staff ▤ had only four lines.)

UT: the old name for "do," the first syllable of Guido's scale.

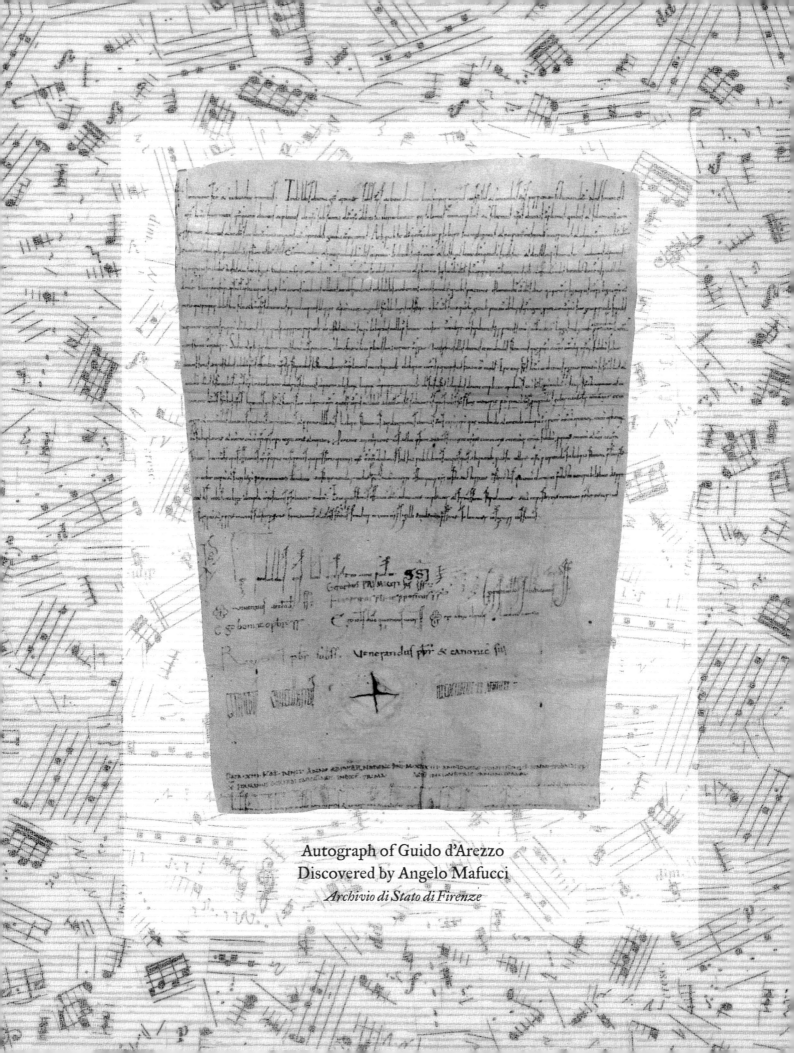

Autograph of Guido d'Arezzo
Discovered by Angelo Mafucci
Archivio di Stato di Firenze

Author's Note

· · · · ·

The historical truths of this story come from the books noted in the bibliography, from others too numerous to list, and from my consultations with the scholars also noted here.

In the course of my research I met with Benedictine monks from the monasteries in Pomposa and Arezzo; I touched the walls of the medieval campanile in Pomposa and walked on the remaining stones from Guido's Cathedral of San Donato, in Arezzo. I studied works of art from Guido's time in Italy and elsewhere. I held Guido's *"autografo"* in my own hands.

The following specifics about Guido's life and work are well reported and well documented: Guido d'Arezzo was born in Arezzo in 990. Early on, he encountered interpersonal difficulties as he tried to convince his colleagues in Arezzo of the essential value of a written language for music. Even before Guido worked out the solution to his idea, the others were worried that their jobs might change or even become obsolete should Guido's theories ever reach fruition and become effective and accepted. Guido moved to Pomposa because he lost patience with the rigid thinking of the clergymen in Arezzo, and also because the clergymen were equally impatient with Guido for his incessant preoccupation with his still undefined theory. The monks in Pomposa reacted to Guido and his ideas in the same way that the others in Arezzo had, with the exception of Brother Michele (called Michael in my text for English-language clarity). Michele and Guido were real friends (they stayed in touch through letters after Guido moved back to Arezzo). Even after Guido completed his work, the monks in Pomposa (save Michele) were unwilling to accept his findings. Guido returned to Arezzo after he successfully created his written language of music. The new bishop, Teodaldo, was intrigued by Guido's work and subsequently became Guido's champion. Guido dedicated his treatise, *Micrologus,* to Teodaldo. Guido visited the pope in Rome; the pope then invited Guido to move there, but Guido declined. He returned to Arezzo, where he remained for the rest of his life. Guido d'Arezzo died in Arezzo circa 1050.

——Susan L. Roth

Select Bibliography

· · · · ·

Falchi, Michele. *Studi su Guido Monaco.* 1882.

Holländer, Hans. *The Herbert History of Art and Architecture: Early Medieval.* London: Herbert Press, 1990.

Mafucci, Angelo. "Guido D'Arezzo: I primi venti anni della sua vita." *Rivista internazionale de musica sacra.* Libreria Musicale Italiana, 2000.

——————. "L'autografo di Guido D'Arezzo." *Rivista internazionale de musica sacra.* Libreria Musicale Italiana, 2003.

Parrish, Carl. *The Notation of Medieval Music.* New York: W.W. Norton and Company, 1957.